THIS BOOK BELONGS TO

_____

BRANDENBURG
GATE

The Adventures of
Bella & Harry
Let's Visit Berlin!

Written by
Lisa Manzione

Illustrated by
Kristine Lucco

Bella & Harry, LLC

"Bella, where are you going?
Wait for me!"

"WOW! Bella, what is this?"

"Harry, this is the famous Brandenburg Gate. It is probably the most famous landmark in Berlin. The gate is located a block away from a building called the Reichstag, the German government (or parliament) building. Many people also enjoy walking around the large square behind the gate, called Pariser Platz."

"The gate was ordered to be built by King Frederick William II of Prussia and has been a part of the city's history for more than 200 years. The design of the gate is based on the Acropolis in Athens, Greece. On top of the gate is a Quadriga, a chariot drawn by four horses. Quadrigas symbolize triumph or victory. The goddess Victoria, an iron cross, and a Prussian eagle are also on top of the gate."

"**Prussia,** Bella?
I thought we were in Germany?"

"**Many** years ago, the country that is now called Germany was once part of a place called Prussia. The city of Berlin used to be the capital of Prussia. The Kingdom of Prussia ended in 1918."

"Hmm...."

"**What** is that wonderful smell in the air, Bella? I hope it is lunchtime!"

"Yes, it is, Harry."

"First, we will have bratwurst. Bratwurst is a sausage usually made of veal, pork, or beef and is often fried or grilled. We will also be having Schnitzel Holstein (a breaded cutlet of turkey, veal, pork, or chicken, with fried egg and onion) and Kartoffelpuffer (potato pancakes)!"

"YUMMY! Bella, I think these are some of my favorite foods ever."

"Mine too, Harry!"

11

North Sea

Denmark

Netherlands

Belgium

Berlin

Germany

Luxembourg

France

Czech
Republic

Switzerland

Austria

12

Baltic
Sea

Poland

"**Let's** peek at our map, Harry. We are here. Germany is located on the European continent. There are nine other countries that surround Germany: Austria, Belgium, Czech Republic, Denmark, France, Luxembourg, the Netherlands, Poland, and Switzerland. Berlin is both a city and a state. There are sixteen states in Germany."

"**Germany** has a very long history, Harry. Look over there. That is what is left of the Berlin Wall, a wall that divided the city. The Berlin Wall cut off West Berlin from East Germany (and East Berlin). The Berlin Wall was built in 1961 and it came down in 1989."

"**Our** next stop is Museum Island!
Harry, you know how much I love museums!"

"**Yes,** Bella, I know you love museums, but I have never heard of an island that is a museum!"

"Oh Harry, the island is not a museum. Museum Island is a small piece of land in the city of Berlin that is surrounded by the Spree River. There are five different museums on the island: The Altes Museum, Neues Museum, Alte Nationalgalerie, Bode Museum, and the Pergamon Museum."

"**Each** museum holds different types of treasures. My favorite is the Neues Museum. The sculpture of Queen Nefertiti is currently on display there."

"Remember, Harry? We learned about her when we visited Cairo."

"YES! I remember, Bella."

19

"**Off** we go, Harry. We are boarding a riverboat with our family. We are going to take a cruise on the Spree River. This is a great way to see some of the sights of Berlin."

"Bella, who lives in that big house, with the pretty gardens, just past the bridge?"

"That is Charlottenburg Palace. It is the biggest palace in Berlin. No one lives in the palace now, but people can visit the grounds and some of the palace buildings. Let's get off the boat so we can tour the palace and play in the gardens."

"Let's play chase, Bella! You're it!"

"**Faster,** Bella! Faster!"

Harry was not paying attention while he was running and suddenly a large lake appeared!

"Harry, put on your puppy brakes!" Bella shouted.

23

"**Whoa!** Where did this lake come from?"

"Ha! Ha! Harry, this is the Carp Pond on the palace grounds. It is filled with carp (fish). It's a good thing you didn't fall in! The fish would have nibbled on your paws!"

24

"**That** was a lot of fun, Harry, but our family is leaving the palace. We are off to see more sights and sounds of Germany!"

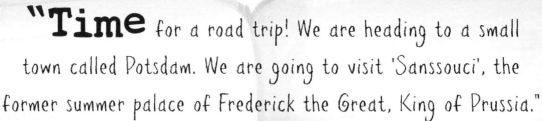

"**Time** for a road trip! We are heading to a small town called Potsdam. We are going to visit 'Sanssouci', the former summer palace of Frederick the Great, King of Prussia."

"Bella, who was Frederick the Great?"

"**Frederick** the Great (or Frederick II) was a great leader and many people believe he made Germany a stronger country."

"**Frederick** the Great did a lot of great things like making his kingdom bigger and introducing new foods, like turnips and potatoes."

"Yummy! I love potatoes."

"I know, Harry!"

"He also loved the French style of building. Sanssouci is built in the Rococo style but it is said Frederick the Great loved his doggies most of all!"

30

Well, we had a great time in Berlin, Germany! We hope you join us for our next adventure, but for now it's good-bye, or "auf Wiedersehen," from Bella Boo and Harry too!

32

Our Adventure to Berlin

Bella and Harry enjoying a pretzel.

Bella and Harry looking at the Ampelmännchen
(little traffic light man) before crossing the street.

Bella and Harry at the Holocaust Memorial.

Bella and Harry standing in front of the Reichstag.

Common German Words

Hallo – Hello

Auf Wiedersehen – Good-bye

Danke – Thank you

Ja – Yes

Nein – No

Guten Morgen – Good Morning

Guten Abend – Good Evening

Requests for permission to make copies of any part of the work should be directed to BellaAndHarryGo@aol.com or 855-235-5211.

Library of Congress Cataloging-in-Publications Data is available

Manzione, Lisa

The Adventures of Bella & Harry: Let's Visit Berlin!

ISBN: 978-1-937616-55-7

First Edition

Book Fifteen of Bella & Harry Series

For further information please visit:

BellaAndHarry.com

or

Email: BellaAndHarryGo@aol.com

Printed in the United States of America

Phoenix Color, Hagerstown, Maryland

February 2015

15 2 15 PC 1 1